SIEGE AT RIO BEND

PEDRO LEON

BALBOA.PRESS

A DIVISION OF HAY HOUSE

Balboa Press books may be ordered through
booksellers or by contacting:

Balboa Press
A Division of Hay House
1663 Liberty Drive
Bloomington, IN 47403
www.balboapress.com
844-682-1282

Because of the dynamic nature of the Internet, any web
addresses or links contained in this book may have changed
since publication and may no longer be valid. The views
expressed in this work are solely those of the author and do
not necessarily reflect the views of the publisher, and the
publisher hereby disclaims any responsibility for them.

The author of this book does not dispense medical advice
or prescribe the use of any technique as a form of treatment
for physical, emotional, or medical problems without the
advice of a physician, either directly or indirectly. The intent
of the author is only to offer information of a general nature
to help you in your quest for emotional and spiritual well-
being. In the event you use any of the information in this book
for yourself, which is your constitutional right, the author and
the publisher assume no responsibility for your actions.

Any people depicted in stock imagery provided
by Getty Images are models, and such images
are being used for illustrative purposes only.
Certain stock imagery © Getty Images.

Print information available on the last page.

ISBN: 978-1-9822-5915-0 (sc)
ISBN: 978-1-9822-5916-7 (e)

Balboa Press rev. date: 11/18/2020

ACKNOWLEDGMENT

First of all I would like to thank mom and dad.

Gloria and Pedro Leon and my stepmother Ignicia Leon and may they rest in peace.

And my mother in law Marcelina Rodriguez.

My wife Lupe Leon for her love,patience and unstanding.

My 3 nephews Aj.Omar and Noelito for there help With my computer problems.

Now to thank all our friends that we have met here in the Imperial Valley and my co workers from ICE in El Centro Ca. And all my Duty stations.

Friends from Las Chabelas, Turi and the crew.

And band members from pure inspiration and The East side brass.

Also, I would like to thank our friends that we have met in our travels. First from Rio Bend RV park and Resort in El Centro Ca.

GARY and Ann from Canada.

Cynthia and Nancy office staff.

Rick and Cathy from Oregon.

Bob and Judy. Golf course.

Ron and Sharon from Oregon.

Jimmy and Irene.

Alberto and Maria from Rio Bend.

John john from Rio Bend.

Cesar from Selma ca.

Melvin from Best Buy in Santa Clarita Ca.who helped me out with my cellphone problems.

Cattlemans Kountry kitchen in Roswell NM.

Best onion and liver in the world.

And all those snow birds that we met at Rio Bend.

And thank all of yous from the bottom of Our hearts.

Our home is where we park.

G rowing up in the Imperial Valley, I had many opportunities to see various motorhomes, coach buses and RVs. I used to think "what a great way to live and travel." My siblings and I never got to stay at one place year around due to the custody orders between our parents. My brother and I lived with our dad most of the school year and with our mom during the summers. Traveling back and forth, yeah, I wanted that motorhome rule the road kind of life.

Going into the Marines for a four year span, I met a lot of great guys. Sometimes we would talk about what we would do and where we would live when we got out of the Marines. Everyone knew that I wanted to explore the open road. My comrades and I made a promise to visit

when we were all out, and as great as some friendships are, we never did.

However in the military experience I was able to get a get job with the police force. My restless heart wasn't happy. Despite my trying to support a young family, I changed careers to become a long haul truck driver. I enjoyed that no b.s, lots of traveling, seeing those ever magnificent motorhomes and RV, and the work was easy . But that life wasn't good for a married man with kids. After several years, I went into a different kind of law enforcement, Ice Agent.

That seem to suit my family's need better while I still got away....for a while. A wandering soul didn't mean I didn't love my family, but it came at a high price. After twenty-five years of married life, I found myself a single man with grown children. Having paid my dues to my family and country, I felt it was time for my wants to come first.

I remembered those 'almost' promises to myself to get one of those RVs and see sites I had put on my bucket list. So, after securing myself a little motorhome and making the time, awkward transition from

apartment to motorhome, I worked on my dream of looking for adventure.

But I found out it was lonely existence and not what I truly wanted. I became my worst companion. Nightmares soon joined me. The slightest sound would startle me. Sleeping pills and pain pills could allow rest for days, sometimes. But I'm a survivor, and with a look in the mirror, the endless alcohol binges I had become accustomed to, came to an end one day. After the VA confirmed PTSD, my life again changed after 3 yrs. Cleaning myself up, physically and emotionally I moved myself out of what I thought I wanted and back into an apartment.

Life has a way of showing you someone you need to be with, and for me that happened to be a nice lady in my apartment building. After several attempts to gain this beautiful woman's attention, going so far as to even kick a can to do so, I finally asked that lady out. Best decision I ever made after dating for a few months we moved in together. After living together for about a year we decided to get married.

I convinced her to try living in a motor home, or so I thought. That was not only

tough, but stressful. I had painted this amazing portrait of life on the road, but she was worried about leaving her job. If you have ever downsized two apartments into one motor coach, well....yeah... difficulties. And the adjustment period for her was terrible. She was like a lioness, pacing back and forth frustrated.

But of course, starting out, there was, shall I say, maintenance and repair issues and things did get better.

We stayed at quite RV parks and campgrounds sites where there were great attractions and views. She started to see the appeal and adventure we yearned for.

We traveled extensively. Tucson Az.Tomb Stone Az. El Paso Tx. Carlsbad N.M. Roswell N.M. Albuquerque N.M. Williams AZ. Gate way to the Grand Canyon. We stayed in every place for a month. Amazing things to see and do wherever we went. And we both appreciated that we had the flexibility of time and having our mobile home. Most would call us "snow birds" I guess that's as we are both retired by this point, but we weren't the ones from way up north like most snowbirds are. We had grown

up in the southern half of our magnificent country. Still, it was what we gained as a nickname. My bride and I knew our main RVing home was definitely Rio Bend. They hosted welcoming and departing soirees, and no matter your financial worth. After leaving Williams AZ. In mid September We headed back home to Rio Bend in the Imperial Valley. Cynthia was our main contact at the office, she's a great person to deal with. If we had any questions she was there for us. After a while at Rio Bend more and more snow birds started coming in from different parts of the country for winter and some came as far as Canada. We already had a RV parking spot for the winter season and many snow birds started parking the motorhomes all around us and as time went by we got the pleasure of meeting many snow birds. One of the first snow birds that we met were Gary and Ann from Canada. Gary and Ann are great people and as time went on we met more and more snow birds, Rio Bend has a great golf course but due to a back injury golfing is out of the question for me. Rio Bend also had 2 great fishing lakes, now that's great for me.

My wife soon joined the activity center and she met many wonderful ladies, she became very good friends with them. One day while I was out and about I was asked by management if I was interested in a part time security job from 4p to 10p 3 times a week and I said sure. As I rode around in the issued golf cart I met more snow birds and we would talk about where we were from and other things and after a while my wife and I would be invited for some drinks. Soon we were being invited to go and visit them, in their part of the world. It was a great place to be for the winter, great weather daily nice and sunny just the way snow birds like it, plenty of golf and party time.

Soon construction workers started coming in due to a major project in the Valley. Lots of the workers seemed like really cool they would work all day and rest up at knight. Being a security guard I was able to meet most of the construction workers. Some of them would go to the bar and have a few beers then they would go back to their fifth wheelers or motorhomes to rest up for the next day. After a while some of the contract workers

would take there bottle drinks in to the pool and that was a big no no and sings were posted all over the pool about no bottle alcohol drinks allowed in the pool area. I then started to bring this matter to their attention, they seem not to like the idea. One Saturday knight around 945pm the last call for alcohol drinks was given and some of the contract workers wanted to keep on drinking but the bartender told them that the bar closes at 10p, a few of them became disrespectful towards the female bartenders, I received a call from one of the bartenders telling me that some of the contractors were not too happy that they could no longer buy beer at the bar.

I went to the bar and advised the individuals that there was no need to get disrespectful towards the bar tenders and that a report of their actions would be reported to the office management. A few days after that incident there rambunctious drinking became a problem and warranted a little attention. I talked to the contractor supervisor and told him what was going on, he said that he would talk to them in a group and I said ok cool, thank you.Thinking that things would turn

out well. A few days later it was brought to my attention by some snow birds about beer bottles finding broken in the middle of the street in the mornings, after that, graffiti was being found in the men's restroom, not having security cameras posted everywhere it was imposable to know who it was, incidents continued to happen between management personal and some contractors. Some contractors were removed from the RV park due to their actions which didn't stand good with some contract workers. Things kind of settle down but we would still find broken beer bottles in the middle of some streets, there was nothing we could do but just to clean up the mess. The winter season was going by real fast things were coming to an end. In early March a notice came out about the fare well party coming up in a weekend in April. It's when all the snow birds say their goodbye's and everyone comes wearing their best, lots of bling bling.

March came and went real fast everyone started to say good bye before the farewell party. By that time my wife and I met lots of snow birds in some cases we became very close friends we would

talk about everything even some personal matters which you could tell your personal friends. The weekend of the farewell party came, and it was schedule 8p at the portico that Saturday evening, the portico is a huge covered entertainment area with a bar, pool, bandstand, and a nearby food service. Since it was still early in the day, I told my wife that was going to go fishing and the golf course lake that I knew very well being fishing there a many times and that I would be back in time to get ready for the farewell party.

My golf cart was not working that day I forgot to charge it up. Since the lake was about 3 football fields a way from our parking space I decided to walk to it that day and took most of my fishing equipment with me, including my 12" Marine Corps Bowie knife.

The golf course was closed early so everyone could attend the farewell party so that meant that I had the whole lake to myself, and that I didn't have to doge golf balls and the golf marshal wasn't around to kick me out like many times before. The fishing was great, I honestly lost track of time

Calling my wife I apologized and told her was on my way back from the lake. I clicked off, I snatched up all my precious fishing gear and slung it over my shoulder.

Hearing a commotion up at building where the farewell party was going to take place, I paused at the site. Then I moved to hide myself, but in away so I could still see.

I could feel my brows tense as I witnessed several men dressed in black armed with weapons roughing up some of the Rio Bend patrons, I couldn't believe what I seeing.

People were being roughly pushed into the portico by the men at the door. With the wide glass windows facing the lake. I was able to see the patrons being robbed of their finery and jewelry, bound and some gagged. In shock I watched as the first a server and then someone from the kitchen came out to see what was going on but was attacked by the intruders. Where they fell to, I couldn't see, but my anxiety rose.

I called my wife and told her to stay home, turn off all the lights, lock the door, and keep low. I told her not to answer the door for anyone except me, or law

enforcement, and gave her a brief rundown of what I had just seen. She started with rapid fire questions, I told to stay quiet and be safe, that I to get off the phone so I wasn't discovered, and I would see her as soon as I could.

Then, made sure my phone was still in vibrate mode, how I had it when fishing so it wouldn't startle me, and put it in back in its waterproof container. That done, I slid the phone container into one of my fishing shirt pockets.

Keeping myself hidden as best I could, I worked my way a little closer to be sure I knew what was actually going on.

It was bad. People were being battered by rifles and bound with their hands behind their backs. Someone in black was still walking around with a bag and the snowbird and retirees were reluctantly giving up their possesssions. Anyone on a cell phone was hit by their weapons or smacked around. It was definitely a robbery, and all those still coming wouldn't know until it was too late. It looked like there a total of 5 armed men keeping the hostages.

The manicured shrubs and bushes offered me great cover as repositioned

my gear and peered about. Knowing the gear was cumbersome, I slid my fishing gear slowly to the ground and shoved it under some bushes. That done, I looked about to see if I had been spotted.

I noticed one of the perpetrators was coming around the side of the portico, and I would be exposed.

I quickly made my way back down to the dock of the lake, using the bushes to protect me from his view. In a few moments, seeing the armed man striding down the bush laded path, I would be exposed. Carefully and quickly, I moved to the end of the dock and slipped into the water. Holding my breath, I pulled my breath, I pulled my self under the dock support system and came underneath the actual dock. Trying not to disturb the water any more than I had, I waited, keeping my breath shallow. And then I heard someone's booted steps down the dock. My panic turned into the calm military poise I had been trained decades before. Peering through the slats of the wood on the dock, I recognized the man as he took off his ski mask to catch a breeze as one of the contractors that lived a few spaces away from me. Realization hit me like a blow to the gut.

The contractors were robbing us and we were, as evidenced by their attacking people, in real danger.

As the contractor turned hostage taker turned to head back to the facility with his comrades, I slowly peek from under the edge of the dock to watch his progress, He moved toward the gulf outbuildings, checking doors and peering inside the windows. After a few more checks, and a quick glance across the bushes and back toward the dock, he made his way up the path to the portico again. Exhaling the breath I didn't know I was holding, I used the dock to mask my progression back to the shore.

Rushing to the bushes, I pulled out my waterproof phone case and verified it had done its job.

A sound of a gun pop and screams drew my attention. Hustling as best I could without giving away, I made my way to my fishing gear. Grateful my approach hadn't drawn notice, I carefully pulled out my fish stringer cord and fishing scissors should I need before I get to my stashed gear again.

Using the shrubbery along the path, I eased my way closer to the building where those coming for the party were being be

abducted. The armed men were now placed near the wide windows facing the lake. A promise to old protect from all terrorist, foreign or domestic kicked in hard, and that meant I couldn't risk being caught. Keeping low, I brought my cell phone out and called my X-sniper military buddy, Benny, to advise him of what was going on. Our conversation was brief, and hushed, so my position wouldn't be given away. Knowing that it would take local law enforcement arrive, I asked Benny to come over and to bring his sniper rifle and to climb the water tower to cover my back and once he got on site to call 911 and let them know what was going on.

People are getting hurt. So you better hurry.

He replied don't do anything until I get there.

One of the hostage takers looked my way, and I quickly shut off my phone and stored it secure in my front pocket. More shouts erupted and I had that military and Samaritan urge to get involved. These were my neighbors and friends. More than that, it was the right thing to do.

How I longed to know if help was coming or Benny would be. A thought hit me like

lighting striking a flagpole. I jerked my phone out of my pocket and called and called 911 and soon as the stern feminine voice answered,

I dialed for Benny, hoping for a three way call. After briefing 911 operator and having Benny update me on his position, with the border patrol verification needed,

I turned the volume way down and put everyone on speakerphone. Then I put that phone back in its protective case and back in my pocket.

Within minutes, Benny had confirmed that he was on the water tower about 2000 yards from the portico.

And had an Eagle eye on the situation so he could help direct law enforcement when they arrived.

The operator said she would relay information, but Benny and I were not to put ourselves at risk of bodily harm.

Benny then asked for permission to shoot a suspect if need be, Benny was then given the green light to shoot at will. The operator relayed that law enforcement was en route. ETA about 15 minutes.

"Understood," came Benny's tight reply. Followed quickly with, "Scout coming

around the lake side of the facility. Hey Peter better find cover.

Knowing I was vulnerable where I was, and unable to take better cover, I decided to take the offensive and as the armed assailant came around the corner scanning the terrain, I sprang forward and punching him hard in the gut, bringing him up short and out of breath.

Then I punched him as hard as my old Marine fist could.

The crunch of his nose as my knuckles melded with his face, while blood poured from his nose and mouth.

I quickly kicked away his weapon and proceeded to beat him until he was unconscious. Shaking, I checked and saw that with all that commotion inside, my attack had gone unnoticed. Using my fishing scissors, I cut a sleeve from the perpetrators dark jacket and made a gag of it for its owner. I used his own belt to secure his hands behind his back. Then dragged the guy off the path and into the bushes. Successfully maneuvering the man from out of sight, I dropped my head to catch me breath.

A single pop made my head come up in time to see a second construction

worker turned enemy drop yards from my position. The body fell onto the path and a small stream of red trickling from the head wound. My gaze went to the rustic water tower and I gave a mock salute.

I then listen to the relaying of intel via my cell phone as I heaved another form to the bushes out of eyesight of the portico and the windows facing the lake. Wiping my hand across my eye brow, I tried to control my heaving breathing. I came here for a peaceful retirement "I didn't want this kind of adventure ." Closing my eyes, I fought for control of my emotions and my aged body. Hearing more shouts and screams, I exhaled loudly. The sound of a fire arm had me bold for cover. I rushed up to the bushes near the portico's wall and braced myself against A window's framing. In anguish, I washed another neighbor a snow bird, attempting to assist his spouse being hit hard by a rifle coming down hard. I bit into my thumb to prevent from crying out. I barely heard a muffled warning from Benny about more patrols getting ready to search the perimeter of the portico. Nodding, I tried to pull myself together and shift back toward the cover of a bush along the side

of the building. A quick glance through the windows that law enforcement needed to hurry. People, especially seniors, won't last long against these criminals. The operator indicated that reinforcement would be arriving on the scene without sirens to prevent unnecessary attacks on the hostages.

That came with the sound of couple of vehicles coming down the entrance. Peeking from my position, I noted there arrival had not been noticed by the six remaining assailants. Relaying that to my communication comrades,

I felt hope for the first time since I had stumbled onto this scenario. My cell phone vibrated and the display indicated that it was my wife calling. It also showed low battery. I hit to dismiss her incoming check in as my resolve stiffened. Tucking my phone back into my shirt pocket, I grimaced another crack of Benny's rifle echoed a third round. Where was his target? Turning to look, I felt a moment of gratitude and respect mingled with fear as another construction worker with his rifle pointing in my direction dropped lifeless. A quick salute of appreciation

answered by Benny's voice hissing, "you bet. You were a sitting duck". Then his directions and suggestions were being relayed to the operator still with us. I heard the coordination to distract the remaining hostages takers and realized I was stuck in the middle either way. I could move back and watch my neighbors die under duress should the law enforcement initiative go sour, Or I could try and help some more. The lead contractor gone bad seemed to shout at the walkie in his hand. A walkie erupted from the bushes behind me.

Assuming it was one of his partners, I turned it off and cast it besides the corps. Then I looked behind me toward the large portico windows in time to see the leader step up. He started scanning the train and pointed at the door. He used his walkie again. After a few moments that felt like an eternity, he made a face and kicked at something. That was when the criminals realized something was wrong. I knew things could go bad in a hurry. I indicated to my invisible crew that, I was going to sneak into the back door, the employee entrance, of the portico to help incase hostages were to be used for

leverage. Getting the acknowledgement I was hoping for, I moved inside. I was right. The guy I saw talking on the walkie had to be the one in charge. And he wasn't hearing back from his cohorts. He abruptly pulled a nearby hostage to his feet at gun point and started calling out orders to his partners to use snow birds as shields. That wasn't good. When his counterparts started

Man handling the seniors, I moved a bit closer. One of the captives noticed me. Placing my finger to my lips, I indicated for silence. Then shouts and commands erupted from both outside and the building and in.

Using the distraction to my advantage. I tried working out the knots holding the captives. Deciding a blade would be faster, I squatted beside the next hostage and brought out my knife. I tried to cut and work the zip ties at the hostages wrists. Freeze! Drop your weapon," a voice shouted from behind. Not knowing what I was missing, and assuming I was still out of view, I continued to work at the plastic binding the hostages. The distinct pop and pain were instantaneous. With the

realization of what had just happened, I slowly turn my face and face the shooter. My knife dropped from my fingers as I sagged to the floor and looked down. A crimson stream leaked from my body as I scrunched my eyebrows. I opened my mouth to speak but blood came forth instead of words. Those I rescued were feverishly telling the shooter I wasn't one of the hostage takers. My eyes met

Those of the law enforcement officer while realization hit him. He immediately called for medical assistance on his walkie as he quickly knelt to apply pressure to my gunshot wound. His eyes said what his mouth could not.

More law enforcement arrived and started to assist others while I gasped for breath. Hang in there, fella. I am sorry" the young man said as he held my gaze. "hang in there."

As I blinked, I heard my wife's calling for me. The effort to turn her away seemed great. Swallowing seemed easier as she fell to her knees besides me. You'll be ok baby, then she kissed me. And I just smile and closed my eyes.

This is Benny